To Anna,

Fairy Daze
by Carol Keeney

Best Wishes!
Carol Keeney

▼ested Publishing
Monroe, Connecticut

 # Stuff

Fairy Daze
Copyright © 2018 by Carol Keeney

ISBN: 978-0-9752699-2-3

For information:
Carol Keeney
412 Cutlers Farm Rd
Monroe, CT 06468
ck24@sbcglobal.net

Dedication

To my husband for making this book a reality

Acknowledgement

Thank you to Angela Adler for editing much of this book and always encouraging my writing. And, thank you to the Sterling Writing Group for their constuctive listening. A thank you to Zuzu for her cover illustratioon. And, finally a big thank you to my husband Joe for publishing it.

Fairy Sayings

Stories are like fairy gold, the more you give away, the more you have.

~Polly McGuire

Fairies are invisible like angels. But their magic sparkles in nature.

~Lynn Holland

Welcome to the Fair

The wizards were weaving a net. It had to be strong to catch the children who would fly off the water slide. The fair was in one week. Everything had to be perfect.

"I think we should use more seaweed in the thread," said Gus.

"The stronger the better. By the way Sam, where's Jake? He should be helping us with this."

"You know Jake. He is the best

engineer in the village but spends most of his time fooling around. Remember when he turned the clock ahead at the factory and everyone went home early? I hope his boss's reaction taught him a lesson."

"I get it," said Gus. "Well lets just keep working so we can get this done and move on to the raft rides. Maybe Jake will come down later."

Gus and Sam worked for hours. They wanted to finish as much as they could before noon. They had gathered all the materials the night before and piled them up neatly. When they started work, Gus took out the blueprint of the slip and slide he had drawn and made sure they had all the parts they needed. They decided on the steps they would take to build the structure. First, the base had to be rooted deep into the ground to make sure the foundation was strong. After that was in place, they could go ahead with building the slides. Each slide had to be at a certain angle for the ride to be a smooth and easy one. The villagers were relying on their engineering skills to keep the ride safe. Sam and Gus were a good team but wished they had a little more help on this project.

Just then they heard chimes coming from the village green. These bells signaled that it was time for lunch.

"I'm starved," said Gus as he stood up from his stooped position.

"Me too," said Sam. And he jumped up quickly to join his pal.

"Good afternoon, guys," said Fairy Fae. "We have some great grub for you today. Check out the specials on the slate rock."

7

Sardine Chowder

Rhubarb Salad

topped with Whipped Cream and Raspberries

Cherries Ala Mode

"I'll have all of the above!" said Gus.

"Me too," said Sam. "All that work made me hungry!"

"Coming right up! By the way, how's the fair coming? I can't wait to splash down that water slide and feel that chilly water on my face!"

Gus laughed, "And you won't be serving lunch that day, Fae. Lunch will be on us."

Fae smiled but her eyes moved to the wizard who had just come in.

She noticed that Jake was totally clean. He probably had not done even a bit of work this morning. Gus and Sam were just as surprised to see him. He was carrying a tray. Fae wondered what he was up to. "Hi Jake," Fae said with a question in her voice. "What do you have on that tray?"

"Oh, just some mini cupcakes I made last night. They are chocolate and delicious. You might want to add this recipe to your collection. Why don't you try one, Fae?"

"No thanks. I usually feed everyone first and then take the leftovers home for an early dinner."

"Please!" Now Jake was pleading.

Fae smiled. Jake was being kind. She bit into a cupcake but after only two chews her eyes grew wider. She stuck her fingers into her mouth and brought out a black licorice spider. It looked so real that Fae jumped back in disbelief.

"April fool," said Jake.

"Not very funny! And it's not

even April. Why are you such a jokester, Jake? Now sit down and eat your grub like everyone else."

After lunch Jake and Sam headed over to the water slide for a final inspection.

All the slides and dips were in place and they felt proud of their work until they saw the net. It looked like some rabbits or mice had chewed through it. The solution would have been to reweave it but there just wasn't enough time.

Just then they heard something being dragged down the cobblestone path. At first it looked like a walking tablecloth but then they noticed the tiny wizard in the front. It was Jake.

"Hi Jake," said Gus. "We've got a problem here. I think we can't let the children use the slide if the net won't hold them. We'll have to close it down."

"Not so fast", said Jake." I've got an idea. This tablecloth can be used to reinforce the net."

"Where did you get that?" asked Sam.

"Oh, some kids left it behind at the picnic grove last weekend. I guess they left in a hurry. I figured I'd drag it home with me and I'm glad I did. It will come in handy now."

The three wizards worked together. This time Jake took charge giving directions to Sam and Gus. "Listen, I know you think I'm a jokester but there are some things I take very seriously, like safety."

"Boy, Jake," said Sam, "It looks like this will work nicely. Who would have thought that a tablecloth could be turned into a liner for our slip and slide! What other treasures have you hoarded away in your house?"

"You'll have to come over and see. I find that most of the things I've gathered either come in handy or can be upcycled to be used for other purposes."

"I think you have a great imagination, Jake. I see a tablecloth and it's just a tablecloth!"

"We can all learn from each other, Sam. I guess I'm learning too today, about teamwork."

The fair opened early the next day. As Gus, Sam, and Jake looked up at the slide they had built they burst out laughing. Fae and the pixies slipped and dipped down the water slide and flopped and flipped into the air headed into the net. The builders' eyes followed each one carefully as they landed softly onto the woven vines and frog mesh and a red checkered table cloth.

Baubles and Beads

Fae perched on the top of a bright pink tulip and looked up to watch the children play. Soon their mom called them to eat their lunch.

"Wow, barbecue chicken! What a great picnic!" yelled a little boy. Fae had to admit it did smell good! After eating, the two little girls grabbed a colorful beach towel and spread it out on the grass. Fae tuned in on their conversation.

13

"We're making fobs today! We can string beads in a pretty pattern and add a clasp at the end of it. It can be a keychain or even a decoration for our locker."

The younger girl was holding the baggie filled with beads and her eyes settled on a pretty glass bead. "Oh, I love this rainbow bead! Can I have this one?"

"Sure, take whatever beads you want. I have plenty more at home."

The girls spent a long time choosing and stringing their beads on a wire. The older girl took her time showing her friend just how to choose the right length wire and tie a knot on the end of it. She talked about other fobs she had made and told her which colored beads looked good together. Fae heard the girl explain about patterns of beads and watched to learn what she was talking about.

All at once they heard a crash of thunder. The mom called, "Quick girls, gather up your things. We should leave the park. We don't want to get hit by lightning."

The girls jumped up, grabbed their crafts and picked up loose beads they could see. Next, one of the girls bunched up the towel and they both ran to catch up with the family and everyone leaving the park. Thunder bolts boomed, followed by bright flashes of lightning. Then the pouring rain beat down on the picnic grove soaking anything that had been left behind.

Fae folded the petals of the flower over her and waited out the storm. When the rain finally stopped, she uncovered herself to see a beautiful sunny day. She jumped down from her flower and looked around the wet grass to try and find a few beads the girls may have left behind. One by one, she spotted the tiny white beads, bigger pink beads and a few glass rainbow beads. Fae was glad she had worn her fairy apron. She laid it on the grass and slowly pushed each one onto it.

When Fae was sure she had found most of the beads, she called for the nearby robins to help her. "Would you please carry these beads to Wizard Will in the village?" They agreed, and Fae headed straight to Will's workshop.

Will was sitting at his work-bench when Fae arrived. Fae wondered where Will's son was. Why wasn't he helping his Dad?

"Hi Will. Did the robins deliver a sack of beads to you this morning?"

As a matter of fact, I noticed a delivery outside my door. What did you send me, Fae?"

"Oh, some colorful beads I found in the picnic grove yesterday."

Will jumped off his stool to look. "Wow, what a treasure you've found, Fae, and each one of these can be turned into tiny trinkets or fairy dust. How can I repay you?"

"You really don't have to pay me anything, but I would love one of your beautiful heart lockets."

"I'd love to make you one, Fae."

"Will, where's your son? I expected to see him working beside you."

Will sighed. "Jack thinks this work is boring. He's been hanging out with Gus and Sam these days. Maybe he'll be a builder. I'd like to see him happy with his work."

"But isn't this a lot of work for you to do alone, Will?"

"Tell the truth, Fae, I'd like to hire an apprentice who enjoys gemology."

"I have an idea Will. I've just opened a little shop in my restaurant. Why don't you set up some of your jewelry and I can find some customers who love your work? One of them might want to learn your craft."

"Gee Fae, that sounds like a great idea! I bet they'd love a little shopping after their meal. Its fun to stay a while and walk off all that delicious food!"

Fae laughed, "Thanks for the compliment, Will. I thought of the boutique because I see we have so many beautiful crafters around the village. It gives everyone an opportunity to share their wares. I also make bundles of my thimble cakes and decorate them with colorful ribbons. There are tiny vases and trays made entirely from our tooth collections. Your trinkets and fairy dust will be a nice addition. Only the wizards can make the magical dust the tooth fairies need. Finding that a tooth fairy has visited is one of the biggest joys for children losing their baby teeth. I've heard them giggle and scream while telling their parents about the fairy's visit!"

On Saturday, Fae decided to host a tea party. She covered each table with a white handkerchief. She added a lovely cup and saucer to each place setting. In the center of each table stood a three-tiered cake plate. She wrote the menu on her slate:

Strawberry scones
Cucumber sandwiches
Chocolate fudge

After lunch many of the fairies and wizards strolled around Fae's boutique.

Lisa held a turquoise earring up to her ear to show her friend.

"Turquoise is a beautiful mineral stone that has been used in jewelry for hundreds of years."

Fae joined the conversation. "Excuse me, I couldn't help but hear you admiring the turquoise gemstone. My friend Will the Wizard makes all kinds of jewelry at his workshop. He's looking for an apprentice. Would you be interested?"

"Sure!" Lisa answered immediately. "I'm actually a tooth fairy and can always use more treasures and pixie dust for my travels."

Fae and Lisa planned to meet up at Will's workshop during the week. Fae smiled. Her boutique of baubles and beads had led her to finding an apprentice for Will.

Rafting

Abbie is a busy fairy. She flies here, there, and everywhere collecting baby teeth for her village. Sometimes she finds the tooth easily because it's been tucked neatly in a small tooth fairy pillow. Sometimes, it takes a few more seconds to swipe her hand under a pillowcase to find it. Last night, a little boy named Josh left his tooth in a small bag.

Abbie took the little package

and stuffed it into her pouch. She smiled and sprinkled her magical dust on Josh before flying home.

The next day was Abbie's day off and she was spending it at the fair. She and Lisa decided to enjoy a raft ride together. As they walked out on the dock, they saw a raft hooked up to two sparkling pink seahorses. They noticed other rafts being pulled around the lake.

"Watch your step getting in," Gus warned, as he held out his hand to help Abbie and Lisa climb onto the raft. "Sit quickly, please." He motioned to the seahorses to begin their ride. Abbie turned to Lisa and began chatting. She noticed that Lisa was wearing a beautiful heart locket that sparkled in the sunlight.

"What a beautiful necklace, Lisa. Where did you get it?"

Lisa explained her good fortune

to get a job learning gemology from Wizard Will. "He said I can keep all the grains of metal and stones and keep them for pixie dust. I promise to save some for you too, Abbie."

"Thank you, Lisa, I can always use some more pixie dust for my travels. I'm happy you are making jewelry with Wizard Will. I like to be creative too, but I think singing is what I love to do! I visited a little girl in Windsor last night. When I flew in the window, she was awake and singing a sweet song that her mother must have taught her. I stood on her bedpost and listened until she fell asleep."

Lullaby and good night
In the skies stars are bright
May the moons silvery beam
Bring you sweet dreams

Abbie explained that this wasn't

the first time she had heard the little girl singing that song. On another visit, the girl's mom had taught her the words of the song she called the Brahm's lullaby. "I can see that this soft song would help you fall asleep and have sweet dreams too."

Suddenly, Abbie jumped up and continued singing. "Sit down, Abbie!" yelled Lisa. The raft tilted to one side. Lisa tried to grab Abbie's hand, but it was too late. Abbie splashed into the water so fast, she didn't even have a chance to fly. Lisa thought fast. She unhooked the seahorses from the raft and yelled for them to help Abbie. One of them rushed over so Abbie so she could grab his rein. The other one swam under Abbie and got her onto his back. Abbie coughed the water out of her lung and held tightly to the seahorse's neck. Once he saw Abbie was safe, the first seahorse swam over to save Lisa.

Abbie, Lisa and their seahorses headed for shore One seahorse spoke, "Let's get you two to safety and we'll worry about the raft later." Everyone in the village had lined up to see the dramatic rescue. They cheered when the seahorses deposited both the fairies on shore. Gus was the first to greet them. He had seen Abbie standing and singing and knew that performance had led to the accident. While others took care of the exhausted seahorses and planned to bring in the raft, Gus spoke to the fairies. "We put these chairs out for both of you to rest and we'll get you some juice. "Someone offered towels to the fairies, so they could dry off.

Abbie spoke first, "Sorry, Gus, I

couldn't help myself. I just wanted to sing that song and didn't think of the danger."

Lisa was wrapped in a thick turquoise towel. "You really scared me Abbie. Thank goodness the seahorses came to our rescue." Gus listened patiently. He wanted Abbie to keep singing but never wanted her to put herself or her friend in danger of drowning again. He chose his words carefully, "Well Abbie, I have an idea of where you can sing in a much safer place. Would you like to come to the village grotto one evening and sing for everyone?"

Abbie couldn't believe her ears. She was going to have the opportunity to sing for the whole fairy village. "I'd love to sing for everyone one day. Thank you, Gus!" Abbie smiled, closed her eyes a moment and hummed the Brahm's lullaby to herself.

Abbie and Lisa spent the next few hours resting. It was a valuable time for Abbie to think and plan what songs she would share at the grotto. Lisa told Abbie she would share any songs she learned from her travels. Soon Abbie would have a collection to choose from.

Lisa remembered what had happened. "Isn't it funny that you were singing a peaceful lullaby when you stood on the raft. That ride turned out to be the opposite of peaceful!"

"Well, I won't be singing that song or any other song on a raft ride again, said Abbie. I'm sorry, Lisa. Would you like to take another raft ride with me today? I promise not to stand up and tilt the raft again."

Lisa took a moment to answer. "Maybe another time, Abbie. Why don't we just relax on shore today and plan your big concert for the grotto. "Maybe you can wear my locket when you sing."

Abbie admitted she would like that. Who would have known that a raft ride would have led to Gus's invitation to sing in front of the whole village! Abbie was so relieved it had worked out that way.

Fairy Mae

"Let me adjust your belt," said Fairy Mae's mom. "You want to look your best for tonight's fair."

"Thanks Mom. And I want to wear my pretty shell necklace that I got last summer." Mae carefully untangled it from others in the wicker basket and gave it to her mom. Mom remembered the necklace. "This is the one we got from Wizard Will. Turn around and I'll fasten it on your neck. I'm so glad last night's storm is over. It's such a sunny day for the fair!"

"Thank you for letting me ride my unicorn today. I will feel very proud riding him. Tahlia will be taking her unicorn too."

"I hope you've already decorated Simon. He's such a handsome unicorn, he'll probably even win a prize at the fair."

"I sure did," said Mae. "Let me show you."

Mae took her mom's hand and they headed out of the acorn hut to the stable structure in the grass. Simon was all ready for his big day. He wore a woven saddle decorated with gold and silver threads. Purple and pink ribbons spun from the bottom up to the tip of his horn. Finally, Mae had added a lime green hair tie and pom pom to his tail.

"Wow, just beautiful. Now let me boost you up on your saddle. You two will be elegant as you trot to the fair. Give me a kiss and be on your way. I'm sure Tahlia is waiting for you to call for her."

Mae rode down the path for a few miles thinking about the fair.

Soon she spotted Tahlia's house.

When they arrived, Mae jumped off Simon and rang the doorbell. Tahlia answered the door wearing a white T shirt and jeans. She wore a leather headband. Peacock feathers draped the side of her face, falling softly on her shoulder.

"Didn't you dress up?" Mae sounded annoyed.

"I think I look great! I think YOU overdid it. You look like that bride doll on the cake we saw in the grotto last summer." Mae felt badly about Tahlia's remark, but she tried not to show it.

"Well, let's get going," said Tahlia. She walked over to her unicorn who was tied to a nearby post. She jumped on him without even a saddle. Mae took her seat on Simon and the two unicorns trotted down the road side by side. After a while the two girls forgot their conversation and began to get excited again about the day ahead.

But just then Mae felt her unicorn tilt to one side. She looked down and saw that the edge of the dirt road had turned to mud after last night's rain. Simon managed to step on a stone and tilt them back to normal but when he stepped again, a puddle followed. Simon tumbled to one side depositing Mae in the water. Her clothes were drenched, and her feet and arms were covered in soggy mud. Mae placed both hands on the wet ground to boost herself up, but it was too slippery to get a grip.

Tahlia and her unicorn had somehow managed not to fall. They turned back to face Mae. "Give me your hand and I'll pull you up."

"OK, well let me try to get my foot on this rock." Tahlia hoisted Mae up to a standing position. Next, Tahlia tugged on Simon's reins to pull him out of the mud.

Thankful to be on drier ground, but with tears in her eyes she tuned to her friend. "Thanks Tahlia! But look at us now. Simon and I can't go to the fair like this!"

Tahlia had an idea. "Let's go back to my house. You can bathe in the pond and Simon can take a dip too. We might not get to the fair when it opens, but I promise you, we won't miss it."

The water felt great to both Mae and Simon. Tahlia came out of her house carrying a few towels and a tiny burlap bag. "What's in there?" asked Mae.

"It will be your cool new dress. We can cut the bag open, fold it in half and cut a hole on the top for your head."

"I can't picture it, but it sounds good to me." The girls worked together folding and cutting and when it was done, Tahlia lifted the dress over Mae's head and tied some feathers around her waist.

Mae looked down at her dress and smiled. "You're quite a fashion designer, Tahlia."

Now Tahlia reached down into her pocket and offered a couple of baby carrots to the unicorns. Soon the four of them were ready for their journey to the fair.

As they finally approached the fair they could hear the music playing.

The wizards called, "Welcome fairies! We're so happy you made it."

"We had a little accident on the way. We're just so glad we've arrived!"

"You have lots of time to enjoy the rides and fun. Why don't you come with me to the village grotto? You can relax and share a snack and some entertainment."

They both agreed and happily followed the Wizard towards the music. The singer was a familiar tooth fairy. Abbie was singing a pretty lullaby that she had probably heard in her travels. The soothing song was just what Mae and Tahlia needed after their eventful day. They closed their eyes and let the music soothe them.

They looked up to see Fairy Fae offering them a tray filled with fruits and treats. "Oh, thank you so much. Everyone here has been so nice to us."

"We're happy you made it and when the concert is finished, I'll personally show you around the fair. We have plenty of time."

Mae and Tahlia thanked Fairy Fae warmly and then Mae turned to her friend. "I really should be giving you the biggest thanks, Tahlia. You thought quickly and saved the day!"

"I think you would have helped me if I was the one who had fallen in the mud! That's what friends are for."

The Cat

Jake lay down on his belly and placed his ear on the grassy ground, so he could hear the vibration better. Something was walking toward the fair. An animal could stomp out everything that had taken weeks to build. Even their homes weren't safe. He sensed it was getting closer. As he stood up he decided, "I will go out and stop him. It's up to me."

Jake guessed the location of the animal but unfortunately landed in a field too far east. He found himself in a maze of cornfields. There were no animals in sight. He decided to look around in case the cat was hiding but soon lost his way. He felt stuck." Maybe I'll never get out of this maze today." He decided to sit down and work his magic. He took off quickly again without a good plan. This time he landed near a beautiful red windmill. White blades spun around slowly helping to pump water to a nearby field. Jake was disappointed and a little confused. He decided to find a spot to rest inside the windmill but not before he adjusted his hat and transformed himself into human size. He found a soft pile of hay and lay down to sleep for a while. When he finally opened his eyes, a family of field mice were staring at him. The mice had never had the good fortune of meeting a wizard before. They were amazed at his fancy clothes and pointy hat. He seemed to have a little blue dust around him. He certainly didn't look like the farmer who walked in and out of the windmill. Where had he come from?

Jake rubbed his eyes. Was this a family of mice standing in front of him? He sat up and smiled at the mice. "Hi, I'm Wizard Jake and I have flown here to find an animal that seems to be walking toward my village. I thought he lived in a farmhouse nearby. Have you seen any animals wandering around?"

One of the mice remembered a small cat had been prowling around the barn recently. "He didn't seem to have a home to go to. But I don't understand your fear, Mr. Wizard.

A little kitten can cause no harm to a large person like yourself."

Jake explained his magical power to change his size at will. He even gave the mice a demonstration by changing himself to miniature size for a moment and then changing back to human size. The mice squealed with delight. They were amazed!

Wizard Jake spoke about his tiny fairy village which always remained the same size. "If this cat walks into our village he will destroy everything. Right now, we're having a fair and his visit would be a disaster."

One large mouse spoke up, "Hope you keep him away from here!"

The mice seemed to have no solution for the problem but offered Jake a little cheese to nourish him before he continued his hunt for the cat. Jake thanked them and said he must be on his way. When he got outside, he listened carefully to the ground to make a better guess where the cat might be now. He propelled himself to an abandoned barn on the outskirts of a farm. A young cat was lying down inside.

Looking down he shouted, "Where do you live, little kitty?" The kitty was surprised to see the wizard and stared at him. The wizard continued speaking, "I see you wear a collar, do you live on this farm?"

The cat stood up and answered softly. "Yes, I used to live in that farmhouse over there. My farmer got sick this past winter, and he could barely take care of himself, let alone take care of me. When spring came, he told me that I would have to leave. He couldn't afford to feed me. It's been very hard on me. Where do you live?"

"My fairy village is not far from here. Everyone in the village is tiny."

"You don't look tiny yourself, Mr. Wizard."

"Well, I can make myself bigger or smaller at any time ." The wizard said proudly. And just as he said those words, a magical idea popped into his head. "If you would like, I would be happy to make you tiny so that you might come to our village and find a forever home. I know it's a big decision for you so please take your time before you say yes or no. Please understand that the only reason you can't come to my village now is that you could crush the villagers with your paws."

The kitten did not know what life would be like in the fairy village, but he knew he would have a tough time growing up alone as a stray cat. Each day he would have to hunt for food and shelter all by himself. He agreed to become tiny. Jake assured the cat that he would be happy to bring him back to the farm and return him to his original size if he wasn't happy in the village.

With a few words and some pixie dust it was done. Seconds later Jake was looking at Gus standing at the village border. The tiny kitten was hidden in Jake's tiny pocket.

"Where have you been, Jake? You disappeared early this morning. Is everything okay?"

"I've been on quite an adventure, Gus. I want to tell you all about it, but it will have to wait for later. I need some rest right now."

Jake walked to his cottage and opened the door. Once inside, he took the tiny kitten out of his pocket and placed him on a comfy pillow. Next, he fixed a little dinner for both of them. He gave the kitten a bit of water. "Soon I'll introduce you to all my friends in the village. But, rest now my friend, you're home."

Barney's Home

Jake enjoyed having a cat for a friend. One morning, while they were eating breakfast, Jake asked the cat what he would like to be called. The cat had never had a name and asked Jake to suggest one. Jake thought about how he had first seen the cat in a barn.

"I have an idea, why don't I call you Barney. We can always remember that our friendship began in that barn. The cat agreed. From then on, he would be known as Barney. He was a house cat now.

He purred just knowing he had a warm bed and decent food. They enjoyed playing games together. Jake tied a rope to the end of a twig. On the other end, he fastened a large clam shell. Barney had fun leaping and pouncing on the shell as Jake offered it and then pulled it away. Jake laughed, and Barney squealed with delight.

Slowly, Jake introduced his friends to Barney. He invited Gus and Fae to his house one evening and told them the amazing story of how his hunt to capture a cat had turned into an opportunity to find a new friend. When Fae got to know Barney, she suggested Jake go back and find one more cat who might want to come home with him. She reasoned that if Barney had a friend, he wouldn't be lonely if Jake went out during the day.

During the next few months, Jake introduced everyone in the village to Barney. They all loved him! Many of the fairies asked Jake to bring home a cat for their families too.

"If you can change the size of Barney, couldn't you change the size of other cats?"

Jake turned to Barney, "What do you think?"

"I'm not sure, Jake. I agreed to this lifestyle change, but I don't know if other barn cats would feel the same way about moving here."

The fairies suggested Barney and Jake travel back to the barn and invite the stray cats. "If they hear how happy you are, they might want to join you."

After a lengthy conversation, Jake and Barney agreed to take the trip and find out. They decided they would leave tomorrow but begged the fairies to understand that the cats may not agree to come back with them to the village.

After breakfast, the next day, Barney jumped into Wizard Jake's lap. Barney closed his eyes and when he opened them they were both back where they had first met, sitting on a bale of hay. "Close your eyes one more time, Barney. I need to make us larger"

"It feels a little weird, Jake. But I understand. If I remained tiny, my friends wouldn't even recognize me."

Just then, a beautiful tabby cat walked into the barn and spoke to Barney. "I don't remember the last time I saw you. Where have you been?"

Barney introduced the tabby cat to Jake and then asked her if she had a little time to hear a long story. "Sure, sounds interesting," the tabby replied.

Jake began by revealing that he was a wizard. He explained that he lived in a tiny fairy village not too far away. "One day I put my ear to the ground and heard an animal walking toward the village. I decided to hunt for the animal and prevent him from stomping on the village. That would have been a disaster. Barney was the cat who had strayed too far from this barn."

"Were you going to hurt him, Jake?"

Jake explained that he didn't want to hurt anyone, just protect his village.

The tabby was confused, "So what was your plan?"

"I guess I didn't really have any other plan except to stop Barney from stomping on our village. I started a conversation with him and we became friends. He told me how hard it was to live without a home. Then I got the idea. I asked him if he was willing to leave the barn. Would he allow me to transform him into a tiny cat, so he could live with me in my tiny house in my tiny village? Of course, I assured him that I would take loving care of him. I would enjoy his company too."

"That's an amazing story, Jake. I see you used your magic to make a cat's life better. That's wonderful." She turned to Barney. "But how do you like your new home, Barney? Are you returning to the barn because you didn't like it there?"

"I'm only here on a mission, tabby cat. I want to offer a new home to you. Jake will take loving care of both of us and the three of us will be friends and family too."

Jake wanted to make sure the

tabby cat would be happy with her decision. "If you don't like living in the village, I will bring you back and return you to your original size."

"That sounds like a great idea, but I can't go anywhere now. I'm busy right now. I'm taking care of a litter of kittens. They're behind the barn. Would you like to meet them?"

The three of them left the barn and followed the tabby cat outside. On the ground was a bundle of kittens, some looked like the tabby cat and others were black and white. Wizard Will produced a baby bottle of milk for each of kittens, while the tabby continued thinking about the offer she had heard.

Finally, she spoke. "It sounds like a wonderful life for me, but I'm afraid I can't abandon these little babies."

Wizard Jake happily explained that other fairies were hoping to adopt a cat too. Each one of the kittens can come with us and find a forever home. It will be a better life for everyone."

Tabby cat didn't have to think too long before she agreed to go home with Jake and Barney. Jake produced a large straw basket and carefully placed each kitten inside. He beckoned Barney and tabby cat to come near the basket and close their eyes. They became tiny in a second and in the next second were sitting by a fireplace in Jake's tiny home. Jake and Barney made sure the tabby cat and all her kittens were comfortable as they lay down for the night. They all fell asleep early, soothed by the sound of purring cats. Tomorrow would be a big adoption day.

State Fair

Gus was standing at the fairy village gate. It was late in the afternoon when he noticed Fae walking toward him. She was carrying something.

"Hi Gus, I've brought you a fruit smoothie. You must be thirsty after standing all day in the hot sun."

"Thanks, Fae!" Gus grabbed the cool drink and gulped it down.

As Gus and Fae stood there it seemed the sun disappeared. They both looked up at the sky but there was not a cloud to be seen. A child's face was staring at them from a foot away.

"Hi little wizard. Hi little fairy. My name is Macy. How are you today?"

Gus responded quickly but spoke to Fae, "Can she really see us?"

"I'm sure she's just making believe that she can!"

Fae decided to respond to the child. "Hi, Macy. I'm Fairy Fae and this is Wizard Gus. We live here in this field. Where do you live?"

"I live in that farmhouse over there. I like your village and it looks very fancy today."

Gus joined into this amazing conversation, "We're having a fair. I wonder why I haven't seen you here before."

Macy explained that she had recently had a birthday and her

parents had given her permission to wander from the house up to the large maple tree. "When I sat on this rock, I bent over and saw your village."

The conversation continued, and all the while Gus and Fae wondered how this little girl could see them. Gus told Macy how he and Sam had worked all year to plan and build the village fair. "Have you ever been to a fair, Macy?"

"Sure, as a matter of fact, I'm going with my parents to the State Fair tomorrow. Would you two like to come along?"

Gus hesitated. Even though this adventure would be a fantastic opportunity to get ideas for next year's fair, it still might be dangerous. Macy sensed their fear and reassured them that they would be fine. "Most people don't believe in fairies, the only one who can see you is me."

Just then Macy's mother called her to hurry back to eat dinner and get to bed early. "Tomorrow will be a big day!"

Macy begged Gus and Fae to jump into her hands and come with her. She promised she would lovingly care for them, they could travel safely in the pouch of her backpack. "You'll have a wonderful time and I'll bring you back safely to this spot when we return."

Gus and Fae looked at each other and nodded. Macy scooped them up gently and ran towards home.

Macy was right. Her Mom and Dad didn't even notice her tiny friends. Even when Macy shared some cheese with them at dinner, her Mom just smiled and said, "Doesn't Macy have a great imagination!"

The next morning Macy helped

pack up the big red truck. The ride to the fair would take a few hours. Mom explained that they would be staying at a hotel for one night before driving home. "I'm packing the clothes that you'll need, and I want you to bring your back pack with your toys, books and IPAD." Macy ran to her room to gather everything. She left space in the front net pouch just for Gus and Fae. They would ride comfortably in there.

The fair was huge! There were colorful tents and rides everywhere. A procession of large animals headed to the lineup for the afternoon parade. Macy's Dad pulled out the map he had gotten at the ticket booth. "Let's sit down and plan our day. What do we want to see?"

"I want to go on the carousel, Macy pleaded."

"I know that's always your favorite ride, so let's go there first."

The carousel was a short walk away. Macy's mom had to admit that this was her favorite ride too. As they stepped on to the merry-go-round, Macy ran to get on a brightly painted pony that seemed to be flying in the air. She thought her tiny friends would enjoy riding up and down and whirling round and round as they heard the happy organ music. Looking out the netting of the backpack, Gus and Fae were mesmerized by the sparkling chandelier of lights hanging from the ceiling. A mirrored core at the center reflected the colors and helped light up the ride. Mom chose a horse with three stable hooves on the floor. Dad sat down in a rainbow- colored sled and grabbed his cell phone to snap pictures of his family. Round and round they rode to the music, until finally the operator slowed the ride down to a full stop.

"Where should we go next, Dad?"

"I thought we'd go over to the rodeo today. It's on the other side of the fair. I see on this map that we can take the skyride over."

Mom was not sure she would enjoy flying over the fair, but Dad convinced her that this ride was safe and relaxing. " The cars hang from a strong steel pulley and allow us to get an aerial view of everything!" Dad was right. From their perch they could see shows going on, people enjoying themselves and lots of birds flying overhead too.

The rodeo was a new attraction to the fair this year. When they walked up to the stadium seats,

Mom and Macy expected to see horses. Instead they saw small dogs running around. Instead of cowboys showing their riding skills, small monkeys were saddled on the backs of the dogs. They jumped over cones and ran through tunnels, as the monkeys squealed with delight. Their excitement was contagious. Macy and her family joined in cheering each performance. Macy held her backpack on her lap so that Gus and Fae could enjoy every minute and from the sounds Macy heard coming from her bag, they loved it.

On the walk back to the gate, they stopped for a sweet treat. Mom bought three frozen bananas and some cold drinks. They sat down near the stand and talked about what a fun time they were having. Macy opened her pouch to share her banana with Gus and

Fae. "Here is a cool treat for you my tiny friends. Once again, Mom turned to Dad and said, "Doesn't Macy have a great imagination!"

Fairy Sayings

Do you believe in fairies? Say quick that you believe. If you believe, clap your hands!

~James M. Barrie

Imagine

The trip to the state fair that Fae and Gus had taken with Macy and her parents had given them ideas for their own village fair. The wizards wanted to remember every little detail of their trip. Sam had an idea, "Why don't we meet each week at the village gate and continue to share what we enjoyed at the fair." Will's son, Jack asked if he could come too. He imagined that one day he'd like to be a builder, he was learning so much from Gus and Sam already.

Each week, Macy, Fae, Gus, Sam, and Jack sat in a circle on the grass and talked. Macy remembered her favorite food at the fair. "I love their funnel cakes!"

Fae thought back about their trip , "I saw that sign on one of the booths. What exactly are they, Macy?"

"They fry up some discs of dough and sprinkle sugar on them. They're delicious!"

Fae thought that did sound good but admitted ice cream was her favorite.

Macy suggested on their next trip to the fair, Fae try an ice cream sandwich. "They take a scoop of ice cold vanilla ice cream and press it between two warm waffles, it's the best!"

Just talking about these deserts

was making Sam hungry. "Do they serve any fun lunch food, Macy?"

Macy went on to talk about corn dogs. "Its really a hot dog covered with fried dough. You can walk around and eat it on a stick. The day I had one, my dad was munching on a scone sandwich stuffed with ham and cheese."

Fae fairy had served scones with butter and jam at her tea parties. "I've never thought of using them as a lunch roll but that sounds wonderful." Fae decided to add this to her menu immediately. "I'm wondering if they sell hot soup at the fair. I often serve a vegetable or bean soup at the restaurant."

Macy remembered the hot chowder she'd tried. I had New England clam chowder at the fair. You can try adding cream to your veggie soup for the same type of taste. I guess the spices they use are important too. I'll look for my mom's recipe and share it with you."

Another time the wizards made sure they brought notebooks to the meeting and asked Macy, Fae and Gus to try and describe again what the skyride looked like so that they could try to recreate it on paper. They drew two towers and a steel pully between them.

Sam had another question, "How did the people ride across the fair?"

Macy described the "cars" that hung from the cables as buckets which were each hooked securely with a heavy chain. Macy had no idea how this was done or what materials would be needed to build this type of ride. "I will search on my computer and copy any information I can find." At the next meeting Macy brought some facts about the history of the skyride she had found on Wikipedia: "The first Sky Ride was an attraction built by an engineering firm Robinson and Steinman, for the Century of Progress 1933 World's Fair in Chicago, Illinois. It described rocket shaped cars which were suspended from the span across a lagoon of water."

Macy had made copies of the photographs too.

Macy research would help them analyze what needed to be done to build a tiny but safe sky ride in the village.

Gus turned to Sam and Jack, "This project will take time, and teamwork."

"Sounds like happy work to me", admitted Sam. Jack agreed! They decided they would aim to have it in place for next year's village fair.

"Any other ideas?" Sam asked.

"We also went to a rodeo," Macy recalled." Instead of horses, they had dogs running around the ring. Monkeys sat on their backs and did rope tricks. At one point a monkey stood up on the saddle and jumped for a hoop that hung from a high pole. He was so cute and when he did this trick, everyone cheered."

Wizard Sam thought out loud, "I'm wondering how we could create a rodeo for our fair."

Macy offered to make a sketch of the monkeys performing their act. Jack said he would like to try and design props for the performance. Gus told Sam they would work together to decide which tiny animals would participate. "Maybe we can find unicorns who would enjoy taking part. Not sure who will ride on their backs, maybe pixie fairies would like to do it."

Fae reminded them that the

first thing that would have to be built was an arena to hold the rodeo. Macy agreed, "And it would have to have a stadium of seats where everyone could enjoy the show."

They needed someone to teach the fairies the tricks, train the unicorns and produce the show. They agreed to ask the other villagers if they would like to be on the team to work to produce a rodeo.

"Well it sounds like we're imagining a few great attractions for next year's fair!" said Fae and opening her cooler offered a thimble of ice cold lemonade to her friends. Macy had brought her own bottle of water but was happy to taste the cool fruity treat. They all agreed to continue the conversation next week.

Fairy Sayings

For it is a true fact that fairies just like people, very often find that a full belly and a good friend are all that they need to be happy.

~William Butler Yeats

Macy's Magic

In the weeks that followed Fay often went to the village gate to meet up with Macy and brought other tooth fairies so that they could get to know her. Lisa came with Fay one day. Macy asked her many questions about the lives of the fairies. "What do you do with all the baby teeth you collect, Lisa?" Lisa explained that she liked to keep one baby tooth from each child she visited. She was learning from

Wizard Will how to make jewelry from them. She liked to give these pretty trinkets to her fairy friends as gifts. Lisa pointed to the locket she was wearing around her neck. "Do you see this, Macy?"

"Yes, it's beautiful, Lisa."

"Wizard Will gave it to me and he taught me how to make another one like it. I gave the one I made to my best friend for her birthday. She liked it so much, she asked me if I could teach her to make another." Lisa took out a tiny notebook of sketches. "I've started drawing designs for different lockets. I share them with Wizard Will. He teaches me how to turn an idea into a real piece of jewelry."

Macy was listening carefully. "I have a notebook of sketches too, but I've never designed anything. I just like to doodle whenever I can."

Lisa encouraged Macy to practice her drawing and just have fun with it. "Maybe one day you too might draw something which you can use in a design."

Lisa went on to explain what else the tooth fairies do with the teeth they collect. "We grind most of them to create pixie dust. Each time we make a visit, we sprinkle these good wishes before leaving."

"Has a child even woken up and seen you, Lisa?"

"All children have an imagination. I can sense their excitement when I enter the bedroom. The other night I saw a tooth fairy storybook opened on the table on a little boy's nightstand. Maybe someone read him the story before bedtime. When he closed his eyes to sleep, I'm sure he was thinking of the fairy. I swiped my hand under his pillow and found a cute little pillow. I looked for the tooth inside but instead I found a slip of paper.

I'M SORRY
I LOST THE TOOTH
HOPE YOU STILL COME TONIGHT
JESSIE

"I'm sure his mom or dad encouraged him to leave such a lovely note. Parents remember visits from the tooth fairy when they were children."

Now Macy's eyes were wide with excitement, "Do you ever have leftover teeth from your travels? I know that each child loses twenty baby teeth."

"Well, that's the most wonderful part, Macy. Whatever teeth that remain are tossed into the night and they become stars. The next time you see them sparkling in the sky, remember that they hold the very magic that is inside of you."

"I didn't know I had magic in

me, Lisa."

"Children are born with lots of dreams. Little by little, as you grow, you will discover your own unique magic. You will decide what you like to do and create in this world."

Macy remembered that earlier today she and her mom were planting flower seeds in the garden. "I always sense a little bit of magic when I see them sprout out of the ground."

"See, you've started already, Macy."

"All my baby teeth have been collected but soon my mom will have another baby girl. In a few short years you may be visiting her quite often."

"That's great Macy. And you will be able to share the excitement with your sister too. After all, you're friends with the tooth fairies."

Macy never forgot what Lisa, had told her. When she went back to school, she always tucked her drawing pad into her backpack. If she had some free time during the school day, she'd take it out and start drawing. She didn't have a plan of what to draw. She just did what Lisa suggested, and had fun with it.

Macy's friends were beginning to talk about joining after school clubs. One of the sports this year was going to be volleyball. Macy had played this game a few times in gym, but she wasn't sure she would like to play it every week. She thought about it a long time before she remembered Lisa's advice to just have fun with it. She would try. The first day wasn't easy. Someone on her team punched the ball towards the net but it landed in front of Macy. She wasn't expecting that to happen so when she raised her hand to hit it over the net, the ball just bounced next to her. Macy heard the other team cheer because they were now winning. Macy thought, "It's all my fault," As she continued to practice, she got better at the game. She found if she kept her eyes on the volleyball every second, she could get ready to do her part in hitting it over the net. One day she slapped the ball just right and it soared to a win. Her friends cheered! Macy felt good to be part of the team.

During the year, it was announced that the drama club would put on a musical like "The Lion King" Macy's friends were excited to dance and sing on stage. Macy wasn't so sure she wanted to sign up. One day she went to the village gate and ran into Lisa, the tooth fairy. She told Lisa about the drama club and how she really didn't want to sing or dance on stage.

"Is there any other way you can take part in the fun, Macy? Think about how the stage will be decorated."

That gave Macy the idea to get involved in designing and creating the set. She could imagine herself painting bright scenery and props. That would be amazing! On Monday, after school, Macy joined the drama club. She told the teacher how she liked to sketch and design.

"Great Macy, you will help us set the jungle scene so that our story will come to life."

It was exciting to see it all come together. On opening night, Macy felt her magic when the audience cheered! The decoration, dancing and singing had all come together to create a thrilling jungle production!

Fairy Sayings

Nothing can be truer than fairy wisdom. It is true as sunbeams.

~Douglas Jerrold
(Specimens of Jerrold's Wit--Fairy Tales)

Vacation

They were eating breakfast when Macy's Dad told her about a short vacation he'd planned. "Mom and I thought we'd all get away for a few days to Maine. We'll get in some beach days before summer is over and enjoy some local adventures. I've been looking through brochures and see we can take a whale watching tour one day."

Macy's Mom seemed just as excited about the trip. "I've already started packing bathing suits, shorts and tops for all of us. We're going to have a wonderful time! Just then Mom noticed Macy's expression "I thought you'd be excited too."

Macy was thinking about her tiny friends. She wanted to tell them about the trip. She was considering inviting them but didn't want to take them to a place she'd never been to herself. "I am excited! And summer's almost over, so it will be fun to visit the ocean. When do we leave?"

Dad said they would leave the next morning. So, that afternoon Macy went down to the village gate and spoke to Gus. "Please tell everyone I am going with my family to the shore. I don't know what it will be like, but I might actually see a whale swimming in the ocean."

Gus thought of his relatives and smiled, "Maybe you will meet my cousins at the beach. The mermaids live there."

Now Macy began to really look forward to this new adventure. She assured Wizard Gus that she would be on the lookout for his cousins.

Dad decided they would leave early in the morning. After a quick breakfast, they packed the trunk with clothes, chairs and beach toys. Mom took some totes and threw in sun tan lotion and lots of towels. They travelled about four hours and finally arrived at the Dolphin Motel. When they got out of the car they could see the beautiful blue ocean not far away. They would park the car and not need it again until they were ready to return home. As they walked toward the office they passed a large pool. Families were swimming together. Two small children were splashing each other and screaming with delight as the chilly water hit their faces. A lifeguard lathered with sunscreen watched over them protectively. He seemed to have a thick stripe of cream on the bridge of his nose.

Once inside the office, the manager gave them a hearty welcome and checked their reservation on her computer screen. "Here are some passes for the pool and don't forget to look at our wall of brochures near the palm plant in the corner. There's plenty to do around here."

Mom and Dad thanked the manager and she directed them to their room.

"It's on the second floor and the staircase is right outside. Your balcony looks out on the pool. Let me know if you need anything else at all."

Dad thought it would be refreshing just to change into their bathing suits and jump into the pool. It had been a long car ride. Within minutes they joined the other families splashing and having fun.

The next day they headed over to the beach. After lunch, Dad pulled out a whale watching brochure and they decided to go over to the dock about three.

The boat heading out to the deep sea held at least fifty passengers and provided seats for all. The captain explained that they were headed east as that was where the whales usually migrated this season. They were especially on the look out for Bonnie, a baby whale that had been born at the nearby aquarium. It had been a year since the aquarium had released her into the ocean. Now they wanted to bring her in for a full medical check up before releasing her back into the ocean again.

No one expected the whales would swim up to the tour boat that day. The captain spotted Bonnie and recorded the longitude and latitude of the spot. Everyone was taking pictures and videos of the amazing mammals. After snapping about ten pictures with her phone, Macy stopped and scrolled down to review them. She couldn't believe what the camera had captured; a mermaid was swimming with the whales! "Look at this picture, Mom."

Mom glanced and agreed that this whale watching trip was great, but she didn't react to the mermaid. Only Macy could see it. The whales seemed to dance for the tourists and then jump and swim away. The captain said he'd hoped they had all enjoyed the journey and that they would join the crew again one day. He suggested that if they were going to be in the area for a few days they might want to visit the Cove Aquarium, right near the dock. It was time to head to shore.

Macy and her family spent the next two days at the pool and at the beach. In the evenings they would walk around the town looking in quaint shop windows, buying novelties or enjoying cold and delicious ice cream cones. Macy chose a small mermaid statue in a shop which looked like the mermaid she had spotted in the ocean. She also thought about Bonnie the whale. She wondered how the aquarium staff were planning to bring her back to shore." Would she be well enough to rejoin her family in the ocean?"

Back at the motel that evening Macy took out her drawing pad and sketched pictures of the whales and the mermaid too. She didn't want to forget any details.

The next morning, they headed home. Mom, Dad and Macy agreed that they had a fun few days. Mom turned to Dad , "I know you want to get on the road, but do you think we can stop at the aquarium and at least ask them how Bonnie the baby whale is doing? I wonder if they picked her up and how her check up went."

Dad agreed to make a quick stop, and Macy was glad.

They drove up to the aquarium and spoke to the guard at the door. He told them that the doors wouldn't open for an hour. When Mom explained their concerns about Bonnie, he was happy to tell them the good news. "Bonnie arrived at the aquarium yesterday and so far, it seems she may be released again very soon. "

"Thank you, said Mom we're so happy to hear that."

Right then and there they decided they would return to the shore next summer. They drove home with happy memories of their ocean vacation.

Fairy Sayings

The fairy poet takes a sheet
of moonbeam, silver white;
His ink is dew from daisies sweet,
His pen a point of light.

~Joyce Kilmer

The fairies break their dances
And leave the printed lawn.

~A.E. Houseman

Mermaid Reunion

Gus enjoyed hearing all about Macy's vacation. "We had so much fun! We swam in the pool and in the ocean. One day we went whale watching on a fishing boat!"

Macy told Gus about the young whale named Bonnie. "She is cared for by the aquarium staff. They released her back into the ocean last summer. She's lived there for about a year. Now, they're planning to capture her again, so that they can check her health."

Gus listened to Macy talk about this other world, the sea . He could picture the beautiful blue ocean and the fishing boat that Macy and her parents had sailed on. He wondered exactly how Bonnie the whale would be safely recaptured and brought into the aquarium. And then he asked again about his cousin. "Did you happen to see any mermaids swimming around, Macy?"

Macy smiled and pulled out her cell phone to show Gus the photos she'd taken. Gus looked at the first one. A mermaid was swimming alongside some whales. Gus was happily surprised. "That's Millie, my cousin! I haven't seen her in many years. It's a gigantic ocean, Macy. I'm surprised you spotted her! I'd love to see her again, but I'm sure I'd never be able to find that location. After all, there are no landmarks in the ocean."

Macy told Gus she remembered two numbers that the captain had called out when the whales were spotted. These numbers were the latitude and longitude on a map and could help them return to that spot at another time. She gave the numbers to Gus. She told him that she had learned the sailors also used a tool to navigate on the sea and find a certain spot.

Gus realized that this information could help him visit Millie. "Thanks, Macy. I will begin my search there."

Macy had a million questions. "Will you go after the fair is over? Will you travel alone?"

Gus said he would decide soon.

That evening, Gus looked at the nautical charts that would help him find Millie. He left the next morning. Closing his eyes, he transported himself in seconds into the deep blue sea . He pulled a raft out of his pocket and inflated it quickly. Jumping in, he sat back to look at the scene around him.

He kept watch all morning. Around noon, he noticed some activity. First, he saw just a fin but then a majestic whale jumped out of the ocean, shooting a fountain of water from her nostrils. Then Gus spotted Millie, the mermaid. He couldn't believe how beautiful she was! Her green scales sparkled in the sunlight. Her red hair cascaded down her back and was adorned with combs made of seashells. Gus called to Millie, but she didn't hear him. Somehow the whale did. She started to swim towards Gus and circle his raft. Millie followed and soon they both were swimming a foot away from Gus.

"Hi Millie! I don't know if you remember me, but I am your cousin, Wizard Gus. My friend Macy saw you swimming here last week and I came to find you."

"I remember you, Gus and it's so nice that you've come to visit. My family will be happy to see you! Today they are sunbathing on a sand dune nearby. I'll pull your raft over to them."

Gus let Millie guide his raft toward the sandy shore and finally he saw Millie's family. As they came closer, Millie's mom called out, "Look, its Millie and she has brought one of our cousins. It looks like Wizard Gus is joining us today!"

When they reached the shore, Gus stepped out of his raft and greeted each of the mermaids. "It's been years since I've seen you and everyone looks exactly the same."

"Well, this is a great day!" agreed Millie and her Mom. Mom suggested she'd love to have Gus stay for dinner or, better yet, spend a day with them under the sea. After all, because they lived so far away from each other, who knows when they would meet again.

Gus agreed. He could breathe under water when necessary and this was a fantastic opportunity to spend a day with his cousins. Leaving his raft on shore, Gus dove with the mermaids into the sea.

That evening, they all enjoyed a feast of lobsters and clams and other delicacies of the sea. They chatted for hours, catching up on all the family news. The mermaids were especially interested in the fairy village and the rides that Gus and Sam had built together. After dinner, the mermaids brought

Gus to a nearby shipwreck. Once inside, they escorted him to a beautiful stateroom. Millie suggested that Gus get some sleep because tomorrow would be a day of fun!

The mermaids woke Gus up early and announced that the scavenger hunt would begin soon. Each contestant would be given a written direction. When they arrived at the designated spot, they would find another direction. Eventually, their search would lead them to a treasure. Whoever reached the treasure first would win. Millie and Gus would be partners.

Their first direction read, "Swim near the sea shore, find a coral home right here, look for the jelly fish."

Gus and Millie found the coral reef easily. They enjoyed

exploring these shallow warm waters of the ocean. They swam around lobsters, clams and even a large octopus. Then they swam near a dangling array of colorful jelly fish. "Which one would hold the next direction?" Just then a rainbow-colored jellyfish floated over to Millie and handed her the next clue.

The directions eventually led Gus and Millie to the treasure, but they were not the first to arrive. They joined in the celebration with the others. Even though they didn't win the prize, swimming the underwater race with a long lost cousins had been a treasure too.

Fairy Garden

Macy enjoyed gardening with her Mom. One day they were pulling out weeds. Macy turned to her mom and asked if she would help her create a fairy garden. Mom knew Macy had a big imagination and knew that fairies were a big part of that world. What she didn't realize was that Macy wanted to create the garden for her tiny friends who lived down by the maple tree. Macy thought her fairy garden could be a resort for them to visit from time to time. Macy's mom was excited, "I think that's a great idea!" We can collect things from around the house and use them to transform a piece of grass into a magical place."

They started by looking around in the shed. Mom picked up an old baking pan. "If we build a garden in here, we can carry it inside when the weather gets bad." Macy's Mom grabbed a bag of soil and some bright green moss from her potter's bench.

"What will we use as a house, Mom?"

Mom turned, "How about this little box that's lying over here? We can turn it upside down, paint it and make it into a cottage."

They got to work immediately. They filled the baking pan with a layer of dirt. They added the green moss all over the top. They placed the box at one end. Macy suggested, "Let's make a painted stone path leading to the cottage."

Mom began choosing stones from a nearby bucket to lay down on the moss. "We can take our time painting each of these and build a colorful display."

Macy was excited, "I can't wait to see our garden completed."

Just then Mom's eyes turned to a large plastic box that had been pushed against a wall. It was labeled, "Christmas." She stooped over, opened the box and began rummaging inside. "I'm looking for that tiny bridge Grandpa used in the winter scene under the Christmas tree. Oh, here it is." She pulled it out and held it up for Macy's approval.

Macy agreed that the bridge would look beautiful in the garden. Mom offered to add some tiny plants around the edges of the pan.

When they had gotten that far, Mom suggested that they each take three rocks to design for the garden. Macy put her share into the front pocket of her jeans. She would begin by painting one later today. "Maybe I'll use red and black paint and turn it into a ladybug," she thought. "I thought the fairies might want a hammock to rest on near a small swimming pool." Macy was thinking out loud.

"Well let's keep these ideas in mind and look around the house for materials we could use. "We'll work on the garden again next weekend and in time it will all come together."

"I think any fairy would be happy to visit our garden, mom. Thanks for your help."

It took a few weeks for Macy and her mom to finish the fairy garden. The day it was completed, Macy ran down to the fairy village to invite a friend to see it. Tooth fairies Lisa and Abbie had just returned from their flights. Macy noticed how tired they looked and decided to invite them for a visit. "That sounds wonderful!" admitted Lisa. Abbie gratefully agreed.

Macy carried the two fairies up the small hill to her home. Sitting on the grass was the sweetest garden they had ever seen. The fairies loved walking over the bridge. On the other side, they saw two hammocks suspended from thin brown twigs. "Can we take our naps here, Macy?"

"Sure!" said Macy as she helped each fairy get comfortable. "While you rest I will sit on that bench and practice my music lessons."

Lisa and Abbie fell asleep to the soft sounds of the flute and napped until the sun was setting.

When Macie brought Lisa and Abbie back to their tiny village, she reminded them they were welcomed back at any time.

Macy's school fair was coming up soon. Her Mom suggested they volunteer together. " I can make a poster of our fairy garden. We can show others how they can make one too."

"That sounds great." agreed Macy." We can also let the kids paint stones at a craft table."

Macy ran to get her sketch pad and flipped it open to share her sketches with her mom. "Why don't I do face painting at the fair."

"These designs are beautiful, Macy. I'm sure everyone will love them."

Macy practiced painting each

day until the fair began. Her mom helped her prepare a chart of assorted designs which the children could choose from.

On the first day of the school fair, many children were interested in Macy and Moms display. They loved the fairy garden and now they had ideas how to create one themselves. Some people sat down and painted their own rock. As the day went on, many lined up to get a chance to have their face painted. Although Macy had many designs to choose from, she found three were most popular. Funny, they were her favorite too: a fairy, a wizard, and a mermaid

Fairy Sayings

Let the little fairy in you fly.

~Rufus Wainwright

About the Author

This is Carol's second book. Her motivation for writing it comes from her interest in Celtic folklore which is rich in fairies and unicorns.

As a lifelong teacher, Carol appreciates the importance of inspiring children to use their imaginations, and she uses fiction as a catalyst for active learning.

Carol is also the author of *Brand New Teacher, How to Guide and Teach the Early Grades Using Scripts.* This helpful guide was inspired by her lifelong career in teaching.